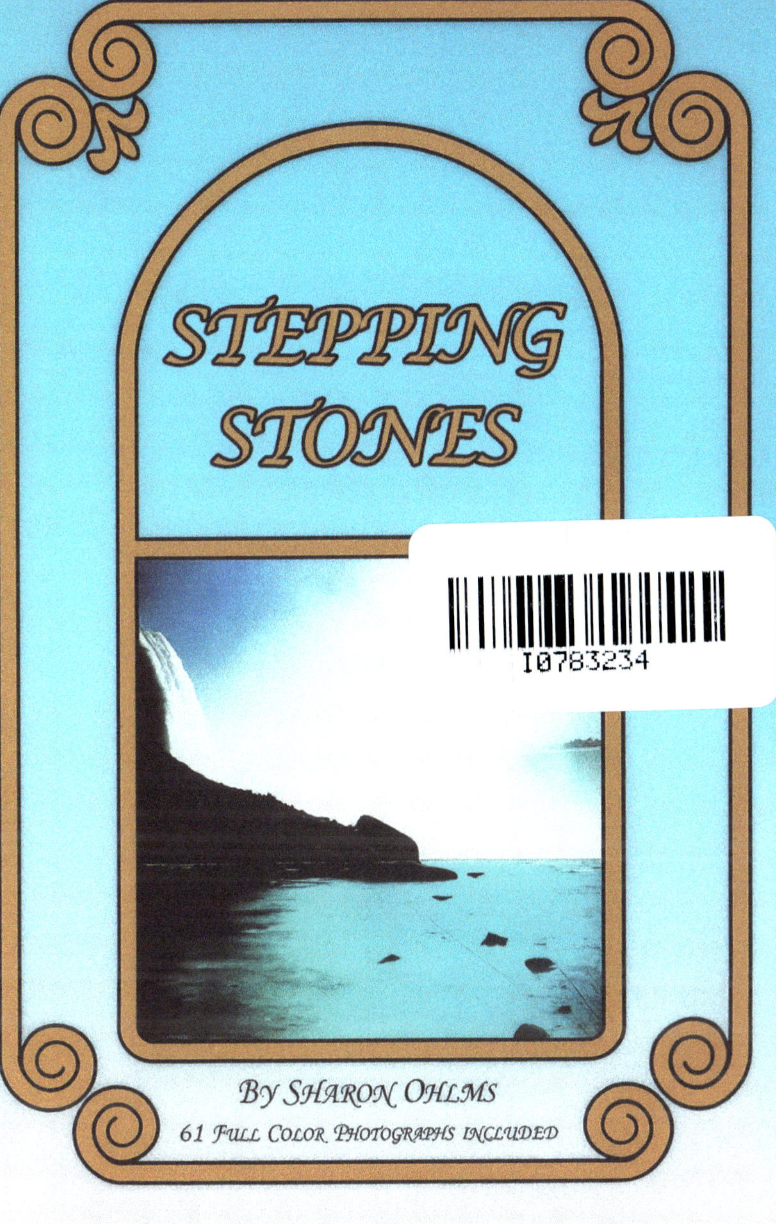

STEPPING STONES

BY SHARON OHLMS

61 FULL COLOR PHOTOGRAPHS INCLUDED

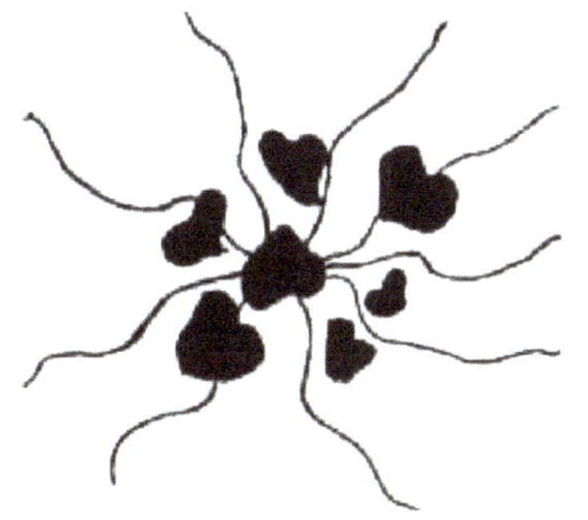

Stepping Stones

Sharon Ohlms

Kravitz and Sons LLC
204 E Arlington Blvd. Suite B
Greenville, NC 27858

Published by Kravitz and Sons LLC.

ISBN: 979-8-89639-618-5 (sc)
ISBN: 979-8-89639-617-8 (e)

Library of Congress Control Number: 2025926098

A Token
Dedicated
To
The Spirit

without which — we are nothing

Contents

List of Photographs

I. On Growth

GROWTH

A young fawn stretches her body
among sunny ferns, also young and newly formed.
On wobbly legs, she nuzzles up to the
earthy objects which surround her, along with their
woody scents of pine and spruce.
As time goes on,
and as her stilty supports become stronger
she ventures out further from her spot,
to explore the unknown.
She stops occasionally to investigate natural scents.
She nibbles at some tender leaf buds; breast buds
of nature, someday to develop into scrub oak petals.
She moves on, feeding on the delicate vegetation,
feeling her body strengthen.
Muscle fibers, tissues, bones become sturdy.
She is now one with her body and soul.
She flicks her white tail, traveling through
unfamiliar territory, then kicks her heels;
soon to disappear in the forest darkness.

HUNTER'S TROPHY
- Next Generation

A round of gunshots pierces the air and echoes in the distance. A young fawn panting heavily is alerted. Ears perked upward, he stands frozen in his tracks. After a while he bravely makes his way down a narrow path to a small clearing and cautiously peers through the brush and undergrowth. His sensitive nose then picks up animal odors as he stumbles over a heap of fur, flesh and blood. He lingers there for awhile, feeling a special closeness to this lifeless form. After some time, he lies down near-by, nestled in between two young trees and slowly rests his head on a bed of needles, strongly scented of sap and pine. The sudden, strenuous run earlier that morning had drained him of energy and now sleep takes over. Nearly an hour has elapsed before the young fawn awakens, partially refreshed but saddened. He gradually lifts his body upward but then lowers his head as if in sorrow. After sometime he eventually again stands erect, his muscle fibers tense, his prominent leg sinews are taut. He flicks up his white tail and bounces toward a scrub oak now golden after the recent autumn frost. He suddenly stops and turns his head in direction of his birth place, to the furry mound of his mother lying in the distance.

The mound remains-

a hunter's trophy never to be found.

(memories of "Bambi" as a child)

Sixteen

I was sixteen
You were the same
We were classmates in school,
teammates in sports,
the bestest of buddies.

Your aim was to go into physical education
mine - physical therapy
We were alike in many ways,
though never physical, I learned of love in
those young years.
We both learned of life.
I finally left my school of 13 years,
graduated with the facts of life,
supposedly knowing who I was and what I was all about,
then was abruptly exposed to the 'real world'.

We separated then.
You went on to college, then married.
I went on to college, then to be alone,
then to be in self conflict, struggle
learning of uncertainty, doubt, insecurity,

still trying to discover

who I am and what I am all about.

<h1 style="text-align:center">Ray — A Sunbeam</h1>

We met in the springtime of our years.
You were in the seminary, studying to be a priest,
I was attracted to your kind and gentle manner.
We spent our time in good ways:
long walks through the woods,
gliding down a slide.
talks around a fire,
sleeping in my father's barn.
We were kindred spirits then.

Years have passed by;
Our closeness drew to an end,
partly because of my immaturity.
But the time we shared
will always be sacred in my thoughts.

Twin Sister

Long ago when we were small
I would call your name
to come run with me in the meadow,
to explore with me in the woods,
to skate with me on the ice covered pond behind our home,
to ride with me on our pony through the hills.

Now the rivers of time have come between us.
Miles of territory separate us, one from another.
Mountains of misunderstanding have built their wall,
and miles of changes sometimes divide our paths.

But still I think of you often
remembering all the good times we shared.
Still I look over grassy fields
and call your name.

Twenty One

You are only twenty one years of age,
a very sensitive young woman.
You had been drinking heavily since noon that day.
Something, someone hurt you very deeply.
you tried to run away that night,
tried to escape and hide yourself in the darkness,
but you were discovered.
And a bottle of Excedrin and alcohol
don't mix well, you know.
Someone has hurt you,
and now you try to hurt yourself.
You have a death wish;
You have no need for life.

But life has a need for you.

*This photo was taken by an
unknown photographer. All
other photos were taken by
Sharon Ohlms.*

A Baby

Tiny toes and fingers
Little kicks and squirms.
Joyful giggles and twinkling eyes
Full of wonder
Full of innocence
Full of love.

To The New Parents

You both now hold a part of you.
Two entities—becoming one;
forming one love
and from that formation
a new formation is born.
From your love
a new being has come into existence.
Your little one will grow
and someday become an adult.
And as you now hold a part of you,
in years to come,
as your child embraces you in times of closeness
she will in that time
hold a part of her.

Youth

O little one
Do you know how much I love you?
Do you have any idea?
And it is so difficult to let go.
But I know that I must.

You are just a young sprout,
A tender blade of grass
Growing in such a big field
trying to poke your nose up
through all the other taller, older grasses.
You try to touch the sun
But you find that you are too short, too young.
You discover that you need to grow more,
become taller and more mature
before you are able to leave the shadow
of the other grasses,
They seem to suffocate you.
You do not mean for them to be cut or injured
but it happens
and the injured ones learn to turn away from your blade.

O little one
Little grass, so green and lovely
when you mature and have grown tall
then they will come closer to you again.

Will this be so?
Or will the other grasses grow even taller?

Maybe closeness—maybe love
will come only with the harvest.

II. On Friendship

G.A.

I would bounce around in her jeep many times
as we viewed the mountain sides back then.
We would spend days lost in the summer air.
She sang of love so freely.
A year flew by
and she was hardly ever seen without her "J" guitar,
a dog named "Blue",
a song in her pocket.
We both grew a lot in that brief time,
she more than I,
as we searched for life - back then.

....

Have you ever found yourself
looking for your wallet
in a demsey dumpster?
Well I have.
And it humbles you.

....

We pushed each other to the limit
to do or die
I did both.

For Hector

I grew very close to you that day.
We spoke of the country, the city,
of mountains, of people, of solitude
of past loves.
We shared each other's warmth.
We slept in each other's sunshine.

Now we are in separate worlds.
You build your wall higher
I try to jump up, to catch a glimpse of you again.
I do not wish to interfere or put demands on you.
I want to be your friend.
Don't shut me out.

In the abstract world, it takes only
a brief time to build a wall.
It takes a lot longer time to tear it down.
I know.
It took me years.

I've been hurt before too,
and sometimes I also get scared.

G.M.

Trips up in the mountain,
camping near the stream,
fires in the night,
walks along the river...
You introduced me to the world of art.
Instructed me in pastels and oils,
lessons on life's canvas.

We hiked the Grand Canyon,
lived many miles together,
learned of a world religion
and grew in our love for one another.

Though we are now separated,
the love will never end
and these things
I will not forget.

A mobile of ships hung above my head.
We would lie there at night and compare ourselves
to that fleet of boats saying:
"We can never get too close to one another
like the ships, to become unbalanced.
It would upset and destroy the fleet and mobile too."
But the irony of the future, I suppose.
That is exactly what we did,
and our world came tumbling down.

Pain

I left the door unlocked for you.
But no one opened it that night.
I sat and waited by the phone.
But no one called.
I searched inside myself for strength.
But no one came to comfort.

And now many days and weeks have passed.
And didn't someone say:
"Time would erase the pain?"

Insecurity – '82

I thought I was a friend to both,
But now I feel as if a scapegoat.
One thinking I was pursuing the other
in their own insecurity.

Doesn't it take more than one to cause this problem?
How can I alone be responsible?
What did I even do?

And I am tired of the accusation.
And of their choice I am a friend to neither.
And what is the true reason for this injustice?

Her exterior was a bit misleading.
And she would exhibit a quick, hot temper.
Stubborn too.
"It was the Aries in her" she would say,
But inside -
she was full of love.

Into my life walked a new friend.
We sped down snowy hills,
flew through pine and spruce,
slid past dips and holes
and worked together, side by side
treating patients, learning new techniques of care.
You, knowing me,
I knowing you,
growing in life.

And I know I won't be alone anymore...
I have a pen.

A Clown

A little toy clown stands in my bedroom.
It was given to me with love.
And now love will take it away.
I suppose you could say
we pushed each other to the limit.

In your possessing character,
I ran.
In my careless nature,
you ran.

I hope this to be a learning experience
and now wonder if our paths will ever cross again.

For nearly six months half a prayer
and a butterfly hung around my neck.
Then the time came I became foolish, restless.
Thought I had found something better.
And it was that very day
my necklace disappeared.

As a patient he was skinny as a rail,
another head injury, caused from a motorcycle accident.
Now he has recovered except for a slight limp
and weak grip in the right extremities.
He can be seen roaming through the hospital halls
now comforting other patients who suffered as he did.
He has come a long way and finally
ended his difficult journey with a visit to his friend,
where he was held in comfort and love.

Sculpture in Sand

An image of Christ kneeling in a grotto.
His sad eyes casted upward.
Wounded hands folded in prayer,
Injured feet pressed to the earth.

And today I feel His agony.

J-

We sat up on a hill that night overlooking the city
below.
Wine, cheese, crackers, yogurt candy
were the ingredients of our dinner,
Love, warmth and gentle words
were the ingredients of the evening.

Is it wrong to continue caring?
Is it wrong to love you even more in the fear of losing
you?
And now that I have lost you,
I will still love.

You were my ship.
I felt so safe and secure in the stormy sea
when you were at my side.

Friend or Foe

You know you opened up a wound I thought had healed.
But then I've discovered that time never erases
the pain completely,
and the scars will remain.
Yes, love can be a battlefield.
And you think you've prepared yourself
armed, psyched and ready for action
alert and cognizant of enemy forces.
But there will always be the sneak attack
and it only takes one hit
one grenade thrown from a hidden dirt trench
that will shatter your life
that will expose your heart
reveal your core.

And then you hear footsteps
running towards your flesh tom body.
And you meditate on last thoughts
wondering if the steps you hear belong to friend
or foe.
And your body aches
Your wounds ooze out sorrow and pain.
Your head throbs as you lie in blood stained dust
And you wish your last wish:
"Oh please, let me die in the arms or my comrade
not at the mercy of the enemy."
Please, be my friend and not my foe.

Bicycles

Somewhere I have felt the sun surrounding my form.
I have known of this radiance and cherished its warmth.
Somewhere I have touched the wind blowing around me;
Speeding down a hill, trees in a blur,
then slowly, laboriously up a crest,
legs in constant rhythm, muscles contact and tighten
to relax again...floating down.

Somewhere I was riding in the country
or was it in a city
and music touched me from all sides.
Somewhere I have touched the water running under me,
pouring over, around and through
and I am floating,
carried past cedars, pinion and spruce.

Somewhere this splendor has touched my spirit
and I have known of its beauty.
Somewhere — but where?
It doesn't really matter-

I was with you.

III. On Suffering

A Quadriplegic

No movement from the neck down.
no sensation either
totally dependent on others for your care.
You cannot eat or scratch your nose or chin.
Someone holds you, but you cannot even feel their touch.
Someone cleans you but you are unaware.
You are stripped of all modesty.
You are angry and afraid.
You are rebellious and rude — before accepting.
You want to die
But there is no way to even put an end to yourself.

But you can cry,
You can think and still love.

ICU Waiting Room

I pass by several times a day.
People of all ages come here.
Some pace the floor,
Others wring their hands in nervousness
while still others attempt to sleep,
their weary bodies slouched in a chair or
stretched out in exhaustion on a couch or piece of floor.
But whatever their bodies are doing,
their eyes all look the same.
And their tired faces exhibit the same flat expression:
That of fear, that of sorrow   - that of love.

The Head Injured

Oh, when will you leave your comatose state?

You are hooked up to a respirator
Your rigid body jerks and twists
Your limbs begin to posture
your eyes roll back
you are now in seizure activity
as your muscles spasm uncontrollably.

Then finally one day
involuntary movements become purposeful ones.
A finger moves in a definite normal pattern.
then an arm and a leg.
You are strapped to a table and tilted upright.
You begin to track with your eyes
then swallow, groan, even breathe on your own.
You will have to learn to speak
to walk and eat all over again.
You will try to remember your past:
your name, your family and friends
And I wonder...

Will you remember - how to love?

The Victim

You lie there so still in your hospital crib -
a victim of child abuse.
Your small arms are bruised.
There is a swollen, red knot on your forehead.
There is a gash near your right eye.
Anger did this to you.
A feeling of power flung its strength at you.
And still you lie there,
unaware of what the world is truly like,
or why this even happened.

Victim #2

You are slightly older now and you can comprehend more.
Then one day it happens to you again.
The evil power returns.
You are pushed, you are forced to the floor.
Your clothes are torn from your being and you experience
pain and fear. You are left feeling degraded, dirty,
sick.
Only this time, you know what has happened.
Not only your body, but your spirit too,
has been tom apart.

Room 219B

The door was shut.
I knocked lightly, but there was no answer.
Slowly, quietly I entered the darkened room.
Flowers surrounded the bed.
The patient appeared to be asleep.
She looked so pale and thin
but also calm and in a deep peace.

I did not wake her,
but cautiously slipped outside the door,
thinking as I left:
that beautiful woman, 35 years of age
will very soon one day
be in eternal peace.

And at that moment
I could not rationalize
if I had just left her bed
or her coffin

as the cancer grew
and continued to eat away to her core.

The Negro

Black is your color,
white is mine.
You became a slave back then
my people owned you.
You were whipped and sometimes chained.
You were forced to work in the fields.
You were sometimes tarred and feathered.
You were ridiculed.
You were not allowed to eat in our dining rooms
You were not allowed to read in our schools
You were hung by a rope to die.

But you are black
and I am white.
My people did this to you.

And who do you think I dispraise?

The Navajo

I see them many times
lying in a gutter, in an alley-way
leaned up against a deserted building
even sleeping in a half-filled dempsey dumpster
always with a bottle in their hand.

Their eyes are cloudy red,
their bodies shaking with the poison,
their minds, in gradual decay
their hearts, forgotten with the past.

Why?

And what can erase this self-destruction?

Jacob
A Burned Victim

You are only six years old,
A victim of fire, heat and insanity.
You undergo months of physical therapy;
sterile whirlpools, painful debridement,
followed by sterile dressing changes.
You appear as a mummy;
so much gauze is wrapped around your dehydrated flesh.
It is extremely difficult for even simple movements,
as you try to bend an elbow or turn your head.
Yes, even your face and neck are burned:
Second, third degree bums over two-thirds of your body!
No one considered you to still be alive.
But you are living proof of miracles.

You are a mass of scars.
You will undergo numerous surgeries,
many requiring skin drafts.
Skin from your thigh will soon be transplanted
to your face, around the orbits,
so you will once again be able to close your eyes for
sleep; the first time in many weeks.
Your muscles are contracting
and if not for the daily, agonizing stretching,
you would lie there in a shriveled ball of pain.

Even still, some tendons may need to be cut,
in order to extend or flex your joints.
And you must wear splints and braces to maintain
the proper position of your extremities.
You will need to exercise daily to strengthen the remaining
musculature. You will need to endure a world of pain,
in just relearning how to walk again.
Every step - stretching out scar tissue,
bearing your body weight on brittle bones.

It is 8 a.m. and once again you are lowered
into the stainless steel tank.
Your tender, draining flesh touches the agitating water.
Old eschar is washed away.
And you scream...
and you scream
louder and louder
trying to cover up the screams you hear inside your
heart,
knowing it was a fire that has maimed you for life.

Knowing it was a fire,
caused by the intentional madness of your
own corrupted father.

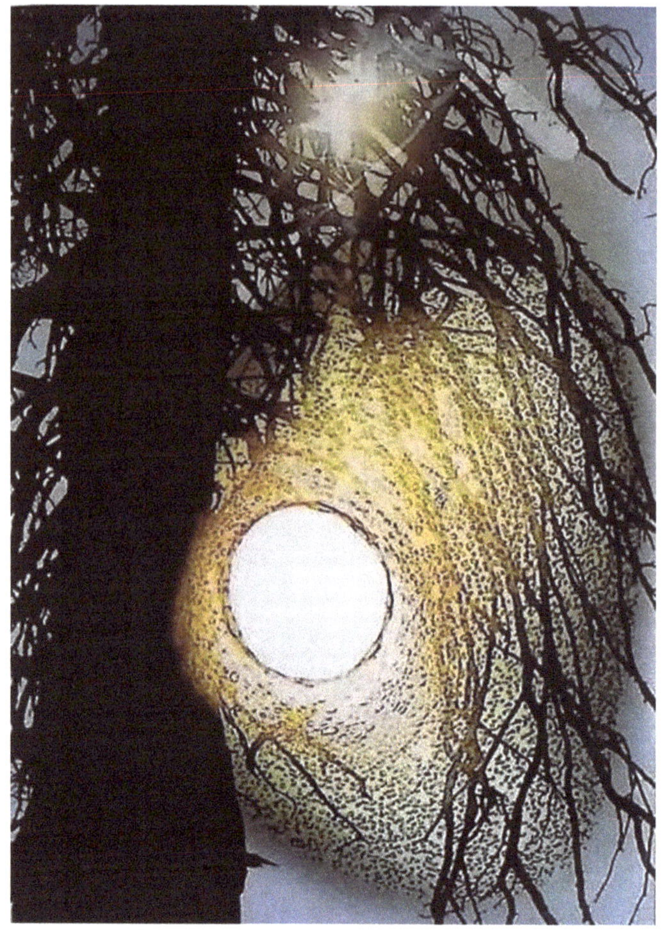

In Memory of Jack

Another victim of cancer.
It had metastasized now to his lung.
The pain increased...
Chemotherapy.
radiation treatments were of no help.
Respiration became labored.

The patient was discharged from the hospital;
sent home to die.
But in the morning of that next week,
they found Jack lying on his bed,
a bullet wound shattering his chest.
the gun still in his hand.

D.W.I.

Yes, you lost your head.
You drank too much that night.
You staggered to your car, got in and started the ignition.
You drove off in high speed through the night.
A sharp curve was right ahead.
Your reflexes were slowed by then;
you found your brakes too late.
You underestimated the approach of that turn.
In just a split second
your car flipped and rolled over the bank.
In the morning you awoke with a severe headache.
You find yourself in a hospital bed.
And then the real awakening!
penetrating - devastating
you cannot move or feel your legs!

The Gas Chambers

Hundreds - no thousands
half starved, homeless people
herded like cattle into huge, cement buildings
never to come out alive.
Bulldozer's
scooping people from the earth
pushing human bodies into the earth's bowels
there to be digested
there to become one with the earth.

The Burning Inferno

You are taken from your homes
You are deprived of your possessions
You are stripped of your freedom
You are raped of your integrity
You are shoved into tiny spaces
You are given no water - no food
You are given no protection
from the heat, the wind or rain
You are left there to die.

But why?

The Camps

The stench,
the filth;
hungry, hollow eyes
lifeless forms
peer behind the bars.

Oh but they aren't finished with you yet.
They will still take
bits and pieces of your body
and make chemical products
of your substance.

And I heard
that in Germany
forty years ago
they made lamp shades
out of human skin!

Your nose is too long.
We measured it
Ten centimeters too long.
The command is:
"You will die."

In the air
one could smell
human flesh
burning.

The Sinner?

You have been severely ridiculed.
They snarl out names to you: "queer," "fag," fairy," "homo,"
You are banned from our churches.
you are deprived of jobs and friends.
Even your parents disown you.
Siblings are distant and resentful.
You are the brunt of anger and indignation
as scornful comments are slung in your face.
Injustices pile one upon another.
You try so desperately to change - to be normal;
Even though a monogamous lover in the past
you now lead a chaste life.
For nearly 7 years you live but are not truly alive.
Even though your previous life style is terminated.
even though there is no longer "the sin"
you are still labeled "a sinner" in this world,
You continue to be a human punching bag in either body or soul.
You are jabbed, you are cut. You are tormented and bruised.
And thinking you are nothing but trash, you are finally killed
either by your own hand or by the hand of your tormentors
either way - you are no more.
You lie there in a heap... You die.

And who may I ask
is the real
"sinner" ?

IV. On Death

On Death

There is such an infinite closeness
of the dead and of the living.
        — renewal
Even under the musty smell of decaying leaves
one finds evidence of the beginnings
of a newly formed mushroom
just pushing its way
through death's matter.

Death —
where spirits merge
and are finally able to be
as one entity.

The leaf,
reposing on the earth —
dead - to its previous existence
still carries the veins of life
supplying yet, the death of another.

And yet
there is such a great need
to be more than just the physical.

As the forest'
a new tree stands
in the absence of another

as in love.

The leaf falling,
shutters in life,
Also in death.

Death -
a state of an infinitude of thought.

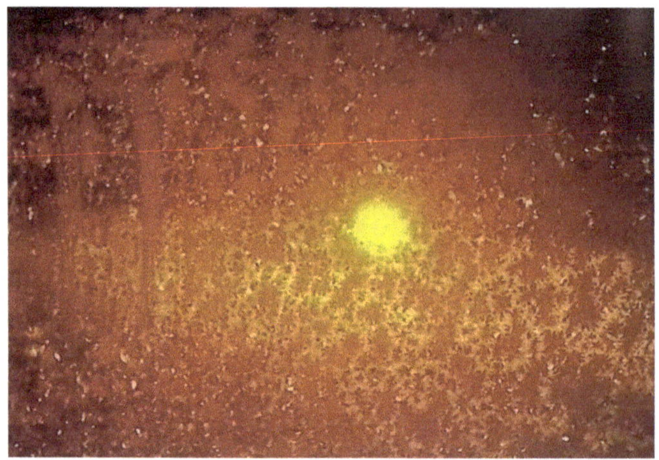

The snowflake:
vapor and cold
becoming crystal,

Warmth and sun,
becoming water,
penetrates the earth
to become atmosphere again.

All in all, one in the same

Life and death.

And unto earth
came the spirit -
The winged melody
of the universe.

Kinnebec Peak - Nov. 1, 1973
Elevation: 11,750 ft.

An old mine,
bottles composed of ice,
propped up on some railroad ties.
leading into a tunnel of dark emptiness.

A mining house
overlooking the vastness of creation.
A multitude of peaks in the distance
and Durango sits snuggled in the hills below my feet.

The warmth of an old tin roof,
the quiet of the day,
no movement to be seen
and now I know what it is to be all soul,
to be alone with God.

Thoughts flash!
Thoughts of a world faith
and of someone I love.

Hours have passed now
and still I lay on the old tin roof.
Suddenly my ears catch the sound of air and wings.
And I see a bird;
A bird which had previously been confined to a cage
- is no longer.

And is it right to even ask:

    Why?

Why can't you boys, you world leaders
play different games?
Choose chess, for instance.
Then you can play with plastic, wood or ivory
and not with people's lives.

Nuclear
Dawn of the Last Day

It sleeps on the horizon.
It devours the earth.
It drinks the sky.
It belches death.

Sorrow is pregnant
Time has delivered
life into death
or is it
Death into Life

In Flight

Frail little bird
your home - Alamosa,
a couple of hundred miles from mine.
Visiting was rare, since you could not drive.
Epilepsy was your cage.
But in the time we shared
we grew close to one another.
We would sing of a world faith.
We danced in the sun;
I picked you a wild flower from the meadow.

Then circumstances kept us apart.
Communication was difficult.
Your cage was pressing in on you.
Your mood changed.
I began to doubt if we would ever be close again.
Your body was being smothered by the cage.
Then right before your spirit too was crushed -
My frail little bird
took his life — now to be free at last.

Time 1968

The weeks turn into months,
The months into years.
Old Mr. Sun marks time on life's highway.
The detours make the road go longer,
But the dead - end is approaching
And time passes on.
No use to try and stop it.
Just make companions with it.
Sow kindness - reap friends.
Plant goodness and peace - harvest love.

Remember today is yesterday's tomorrow.

Willow Spring

That day at willow spring
You sat on a tree limb,
I was on a rock near the water.
I could only see your feet.
Your body was hidden behind the leafy branches.
But at that moment,
Your entire soul was visible to me.

A small ponderosa pine
lay in the water nearby with two small cones attached.
It was still green and alive 'that day'.
I handed it to you with love.

You inspected the twig closely.
There was a small dead part between the cones.
That death was to be my inner core
As we parted -
To be no more.

V. On Life

Chasing Rainbows?

No, maybe just a cloudless sky.
For this time, I will be your sun.
Come sit in my rays; Come lie in my warmth.
Let me comfort you in your journey through the cold.
And as the clouds hide my rays, I pray it will not
rain on you but know that if it does,
the rain will be of my tears. So go your way;
Travel on to another sunny spot.
I do not ask anything in return.
My first feelings of selfish love blurt out:
"But please return again: The clouds
will eventually disappear
and our spot will once again be soaked in
sun and warmth."
But no, I do not ask for anything in return.
I am just grateful and happy that at least for a time
You shared my warmth.

To climb to the highest peak
one's mind must first
descend below its' horizon.

And to reach the very depths of one's existence
one must first know his own life's height.

I could not see
when you asked me
about things along the way—
I was blinded by the pain.

Moisture
becoming atmospheric vapor
becoming the rain
that will once again sprinkle on your lake's surface
becoming one with you again.

A man who seeks truth
is free of all societies and cultures

Loneliness - is ignorance of the Source.

The water swells in its' love,
spilling over the cup's edge
in the heat and intensity of its' life.

then to simmer and become still
pondering life's experience
in gratitude
of all that is natural.

The flower is really in need of the sun.
The sun can give it warmth and life.
It has no special need of a bee.
But the bee needs the flower.

A small female dog lies on a deserted hill.
Her fur, matted and snarled
sticks to the dirt beneath her.
Her stomach moves irregularly with her breathing,
almost convulsing
her leg jerks,
her body heaves.
There is moisture in the corner of her eye.
Perhaps, a pesty gnat
Perhaps because her owners

left her there to die.

Parents—
Your children will flow from your bonds
like the water risen from the lake
over the hold of its' banks,
only in time, to make
yet a stronger bond.

The Queen

I heard something very depressing today;
that a man like you can get up to twenty tricks
a day!

You truly have my sympathy.

Can I help you in your loneliness?
Can I help you in your search of love?

Through The Looking Glass

Who are you?
What are you?
These are the questions you ask of yourself.
The mirror reflects your body image, your physical
being.
But what of the spiritual?
Your feelings, thoughts, sensitivities
Whatever you discover the real "you" to be —
must be natural, must be real.

One must look through the mirror to really see oneself.
And one must never pretend.
Don't ever live your life under false pretenses,
No matter what society thinks.

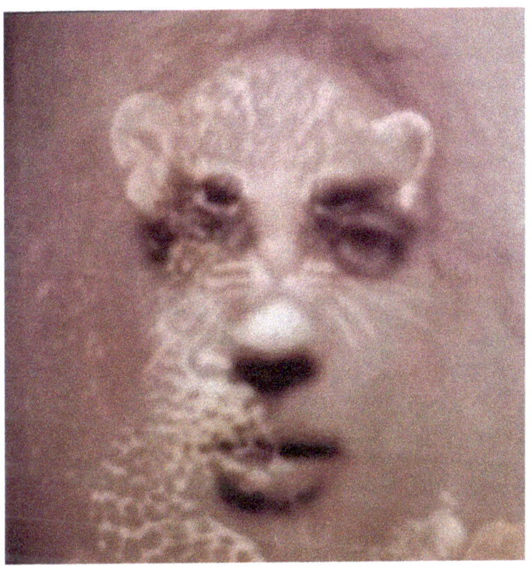

The Fields

The fields call to me in the early morning hours.
I awake
and look out over timothy, alfalfa, clover.
Shovel in hand
I now feel a part of it all
as I open up the waterways,
bringing forth trickling life to the thirsty
earth and grasses
In response, there is a new freshness,
a brighter greenness to the fields.
Soon the harvest will be cut.
The earth will rest
Soon to pour out its' soul again in the spring.

And now in the late evening hours
I rest before sleep takes over.

And now it is I

who calls to the fields.

The song of the rainbow
The sky suspended by mist
The trees bow down
Birds circle overhead
Winds whisper
The crickets sing
The moon softens the forest
And in the next morning
The sun grows in love.

Smiles

Most smiles are of course - happy ones.
It seems they most often appear on children's faces
in times of youthful joy and bliss;
perhaps in observing the smiles and antics of the cheerful
clown, as he works in his profession to produce a smile
to put a smile on every face from youth to adult, to the
old. Smiles from every age
from ever facet of life.

Smiles can speak of love
as in a smile given to a stranger on the street.
Smiles can speak of the presence of God
as in a smile of a mother to her new born child.
Smiles can tell of happiness, peace and contentment.

Smiles -
can hide pain from others.

A Window

We were on our return trip home.
We stopped along the way to have a cup:
tea for you, coffee for me
to view the flowing river
to inspect some sculptures, made of sand
to explore two deserted buildings.

Blue tinted window glass
was found in one of those structures that day.
Stained glass, still left hanging from a shattered
window pane.

You brought out two halves.
One I had given to form a whole circle.

I walked out
with only pieces of the whole.

(Someday I will piece them in my window pain.)

Minds' Eye

Sometimes I think of you
as the eye in the sky
seeing both sides of a mirror
— my mirror
And you've touched by body
with your soul.

Christmas '81

It was a time of rejoicing
a time to be merry
a time to celebrate
a time to love.

But my world turned to pain that day.
Hurt, and others with me too
Family resentment
Disbelief
So potent the ingredients of that Christmas
as to cause my sudden departure.

And now fourteen years have passed
and didn't someone say
Time would ease the pain?

Parting

We will always remember the words we spoke today.
We will think on these things.
And when we said good-bye
You looked so pale and tired.
And when I turned away -1 wondered
When would the sorrow be lifted from my eyes.

I usually
think
of you
in quiet
times
when I'm
all
alone.
Soft
breezes.
The air
filled
with fresh,
gentle
fragrances.

Sweet
memories.

Games

We're not talking about Trivial Pursuit, Monopoly or Poker
We're talking about something that can change your life
and the course of your life, in just seconds.
And yet people play it all the time,
usually in time of conflict, insecurity and doubt.
It is a big gamble, the biggest.
The players are playing for love.

Oh God, they don't know
True love - is not a game.

Wild Things

There is mystery and reverence in wild things.
So natural, so unpredictable
So much beauty to behold.
So gentle, yet so strong
Calming, yet alarming.
Independent of domestic manner.
yet having a civilization, in some ways,
more advanced than humans.
Pretentious - cunning.

Always deal with care.

Wild things can turn on you

Little Child Inside the Man

I see the children playing in the street
playing with their toys:
guns, swords, knives
playing death games.
games of war; of fighting, killing
games probably one day, played in reality.

And do they really know
What lies ahead in store for them?

The Auction

Trapped
Lonely
Poor
Destitute
Hungry
You sell your body
You sell your soul.

And what is the going price for a SOUL?

The Grinding

We parted for the last time.
You ran from the house that night.

I focus on the things you left behind.
Leaving me; still seeing part of you.
My physical now grinding with my emotional
My spiritual grinding me - into sorrow.

The Cocoon

A caterpillar once rested inside my shelter.
She was a fuzzy, squirmy, little critter
Always wiggling; couldn't lie still.
Somewhat impatient in life.
She wasn't the most beautiful of creatures
Big eyes, long hairy body.
Sometimes at night, I would hear her cry.
She so wanted to make something of herself
- to undergo a change
not only in body, but also in spirit.
She longed to be with the sky
- to touch the sun.
She was so tired of being confined to this earth.
She knew there was something better to life.
At times the small caterpillar would cry so incessantly
that the blanket of spun web which surrounded her
became saturated with her tears.
So wet became the cocoon that its' walls began to
weaken.
The structure that supported her whole being began
to deteriorate.
And the little caterpillar became even more fearful
of her fate
But then, a strange, marvelous event occurred.
The glorious day arrived!
Metamorphosis!
The beautiful change,
A change of splendor and grace.
The day she had been waiting for so long.
The time had arrived.
She dropped out of one of the weakened walls of her

shelter.
She left the cocoon
to become the most exotic butterfly to ever behold.
She left her earthly dwelling; she left all limiting
factors.
At last, she was now able
- to be one with the sky
- to touch the sun.

VI. On Love

And if I could;

I would ride the river to your door.
I would change your empty soul into a forest green.
I would change your lonely heart into a sky of blue.
I would change your sorrow into joy,
your pain - into love.

I tried to touch the sun.
but was left hanging by a tear.

Bull Run

A ski run, a place called Purgatory.
I stand at the brink of the headwall,
looking down at the precarious steepness of the mountain.
I glance upward - higher still,
where the mountains make love to the sky.
A sharp pain cuts into my core.
I stand quiet, alone,
contemplating an ended love affair.
Beginning the descent of the slopes
my skis at first grip the snow and
cling to the mountain side.
A strange sensation occurs
as if the mountain is gently breathing
I feel the ground swell beneath my skis.
At first my body flows where previous skiers have
passed.
An overwhelming sensation.
My body in perfect rhythm with the earth.
I feel in ecstasy, as water flowing in a fast current
gravity taking me
winding me across the terrain.
For a second, I think again of the mountains and
sky,
the love place where I long to be.
I feel the presence of my special friend
-to be no more.

I glance upward
A spiritual, emotional pain now merges with a physical
one.
I find myself lost in abrupt, high voltage turbulence.

The mountain heaves,
My skis are now crashing into moguls.
My leg muscles scream, as I try to control my upper
trunk with my lower extremities.
The bindings have snapped,
my feet and legs fly free.
My right side crashes into immense, jagged boulders.
My body is scraped over rough, half hidden stumps.
I ache with pain.
1 feel a snap in my side.
It radiates into my entire being.
I continue to bounce downward.
After a while, my twisted body lies still,
crumpled on a ledge near the bottom.
Except for a broken rib or two, I have survived.
I roll over slowly onto my back.
Opening my eyes, I see the sky; vast, blue, free
with nothing containing it.
I lie there and think.

I have started this day with a broken heart.
I will end this day with the same.

Man of Sorrow

Man of Joy

He is a man of deep sensitivities,
too deep at times
causing him pain and confusion.

He is a kind and gentle man
but does not know where to direct that gentleness
or even how to go about receiving it.

He has been known to drink too much
and exhibit a quick temper.
Stubborn too, at times
but in his depths, a loving, caring person.

He is a man of sorrow
but is known to have a great sense of humor.
He still laughs at times,-a wholesome, robust laugh
and still smiles - a genuine smile.

But in his solitude
I'm sure his face is sometimes streaked with a tear.

He too has been hurt deeply - at one time.

And I Can Remember

Long talks
drinking apricot brandy
listening to Helen Reddy, Donna Summer and Pachebel,
sitting by the river
returning home with a leaf.

Flying a kite to Europe
enjoying sausage, wine and pastries
dreaming along the Rhine and Mosel
visiting castles and relatives
slipping through fields of tulips.

Living in a tent
hunting colored eggs at easter time
building a house, and now a car
lying in the sun - reminiscing.

and still loving.

Truth

Perhaps you didn't lay the paper there on purpose
for me to read.
Perhaps you did write those things in anger.
Why do we always think so badly of each other?
Why do we tear one another apart?
Why do we appear so hateful?
       When in truth -
       We love.

Self Love

Please
Desire not
to possess
For in
possession
is selfishness
and in
your bonds,
the water
will swell
and rise over
its' banks
And in your
pressure - the
glass will
shatter
and cut
the hand
that held
it.

Liquid House

A house
with no strength
no foundation
no love

Aspen

Two aspen trembling in the shadow of a large
granite rock.
pines, swaying softly in the mountain air.
Sunbeams playing on the stones below.
Clouds swiftly cruising the sky overhead
Sounds of water, rolling over rocks, cascading
downward
Splashing the earth
Chipmunks scampering across fallen aspen leaves
and pine needles.

At a secluded pool, water drips down from an
over-hanging rock, rippling the water's surface
A reflection in the pool's edge:

Two hands meet
Slowly almost cautiously
two bodies embrace
Time is spent
Two pair of footprints headed homeward.
two women
two aspen, trembling in the shadow of a large
granite rock.

Room # 206

Blond hair
frail, thin frame
creative, but destructive
quiet, but deceitful
intelligent, but impatient
attractive, but dishonest
    - lonely -

She would main-line
arm and leg veins destroyed
she would use the jugular.
Cocaine, heroine, mushrooms
chemicals were her life
eating away at her.

She would steal for drugs
anything to get high
to escape
to ease the pain
the loneliness.

She was in search of life
but could not find it,
even though it touched her very being.
And now I think of her in sadness
and ask:

Will she ever come to terms with herself?
Will she ever face the truth?
Will she ever discover
    love
to be the real "main line"?

We exchanged many letters
back and forth
while she sat perched in her cage
confined in her cell,
-letters of friendship and love

and the note I write today
is still one of the same.

She spent her time in jail
Farmington, Aztec, Santa Fe pen.
She is now released.

only to be
a prisoner
in her own body.

April 13

Just another day of work for me.
but I am like a robot
I try to make my mind work
but it is definitely somewhere else

- probably with my crumpled heart.

I long to smell the aroma of freshly plowed soil
I long to hear the sound of wind in the wheat.
I long to witness the sun tire in the evening
    - the moon awake at night.

But our love was as a roller coaster
The faster we flew
the more insecure I became.
And then the sharp curve approached
Our love coaster left its' tracks
        spinning in air
        departing from us
        descending

falling in space.

And it's a long way from Denver to Durango.
It's a long time to hang in the sky.

In trying to find "us"
        I lost you.

But you opened up a whole new world for me;
        -that of writing.

to love someone:
        is wanting
        is reaching
        is asking
        is needing

to be loved.

Climbing cautiously up the mountain,
my love waits for the wind.

You wore my favorite shirt that day;
yellow
with puppy paw prints
And it read;
"All you add is love"

Please, let me be the one
to add that ingredient.

I fought love for so long
Didn't think I needed it –

    until it walked away.

1982

You wove sunshine around me like a blanket.
I needed your warmth so desperately
Too much – that time
causing insecurity.
Past loves, past hurt
also causing doubts.

You cried that night
and I misunderstood
You spoke of pain and loss
Again I misunderstood
and ran.

Mow the sunbeams
just bounce against the walls
And we are both in pain
        or
in love.

Love Child

It was said;
> her color is black
> her culture - Spanish
> her speech * white

And yet she was so much more to me.
All colors
all nationalities, all ethnic groups
all languages
rolled up into one.

She was a love-child of the universe
a young fawn in search of life
a wandering soul - in search of love.

And she was the one
who loved the smell
of wet cement
after a summer rain.

And I can remember:

riding on your shoulders that night in the park
swinging together on one seat
balancing on the teeter-totter
watching "Purple Rain"
rolling on a skateboard
wading in a mountain pool
wiping away a tear
rolling in the grass
watching deer play in a meadow

a red rose.

But most of all
I will remember

your smile
the warmth we shared
and the contentment I felt
lying in your arms.

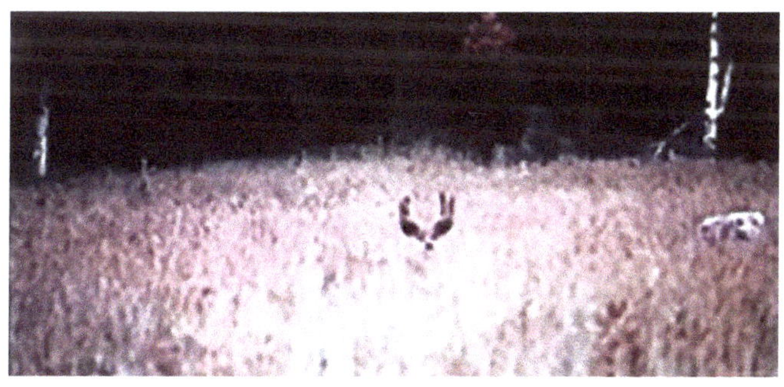

We touched
and I felt the earth move beneath my feet.
I witnessed the flowing river stop in the middle
of its' stream
I saw the moon and the stars fill the sky in the
middle of the day
I viewed snow, softly falling in the air
in the intensity of the day's heat.

I felt this and so much more
all in the warmth of your soul
all in the closeness of your being.

Yes, now I know your name
Then I ask myself:

But what is the color of your skin, your hair.
I think on these things, then gradually remember.
But what of your eyes?
For days, I try to recollect.
Then it comes to me

love is the color of your eyes.

Snow White

And I saw a woman
busy hands
sewing, washing, ironing, working
always helping others
a heart, full of love and kindness
a spirit of a child
curious, inquisitive.
She is the saver of little things
loves to garden
to work with the earth.
Snow white hair
clear, brown eyes
happy eyes
but also sometimes sad
when no one sees.

And I see a mother
whom I love very much.

We are - what we have loved.

The rain was falling round me,
but you turned it into sunshine
and formed a rainbow out of love.

I think of you
as the bittersweet breezes that surround my form.
They whisper in the grasses of the fields
in the branches of the age-old pine and aspen.
They whisper of you
    in the leaves of time.

Hands

So many different kinds of hands:
    smooth, tiny hands of a youth
    rough hands of the blue collar worker
    gloved hands of the surgeon
    earthy, brown hands of the farmer
    shaky hands of one in prayer
    wrinkled hands of the elderly

Hands that move around a clock.

These hands tell of time and love
The time I spend with you.

I know we had some rough times, but:

I will miss you, friend.

Evenings filled with wine and warmth
sitting near your fire.
I would watch you then
snuggled up to a book
your feline pal nearby.

I will miss you friend.

Night times filled with warmth and love
lying in your fire.
I would watch you then
snuggled up to me
so warmly.

I will miss you friend.

Mornings filled with love and sweetness
coffee on the sink
a drive along the wheatfields.

I will miss you friend.

1 saw two yellow roses
in the corner of my eye.
And as a symbol of reward
for a singer on the stage
the final curtain fell before my eyes.

Dewdrops on the grass
raindrops on the leaves
lemon drops on the candy counter
tear drops on my face.

Our blossoms are still clinging to the vine.
Will the time ever come to eat of your fruit
and drink your wine?

The stone of the fruit, as the stone in me does
not wish to be wasted.
The fruit does not wish to rot unnecessarily.

Our tree of love grows on the banks
of the river of pain and sorrow.

A Love Song

I hear the song of a flat stone
skimming, skipping over the water's surface.

You have poured and flung out yourself with love
and have now created me into that song.

The stone in me - my core, my soul
first splashes, causing many ripples on this world's
surface
but then as it sinks to the depths of the river
of life to its' true meaning
it becomes more quiet, still;
almost hovering in the water
pondering over
the love
the beauty

I see
in you.

Waves of water on the ocean
Waves of wind on the fields
Waves of sand on the beach
Waves of clouds on the sky

Waves of love on the horizon.

My tiny wings fly through magic,
the magic of your soul.

O little songbird - take me with you.

Remember -
beneath the frozen snow
lies the beginnings
of a tender blade of grass.

You helped quiet and still my river's tides
after the pain and damage of the storm.

It is time to give into the tide
Set sails to the wind
Give way to the sea
Surrender to the surge of the waves.

It is time to join in the song.
It is time to give in to love.

So take my hand
and walk this land with me.

Take my love
and walk this life with me.

A Heart

Human heart
tossed in the flowing river
dies of thirst.
So many lonely people
afraid to love.
Fears of insecurity, infidelity.
So go on and play your games.

Hearts bump hearts,
bruising in a sea of disguises and deceit.
Hearts thirsting in the sea of life.

Poor human heart
the liquid sea swallows it.

Trust

Only five letters
but such a significant word to hold
It is a necessary ingredient to any lasting relationship.
It is a vital requisite for love.
Without it, there is no power of reliance
- no credence with the truth

Wings

Come with me
and we will make love in the sky.
We will fly together and pattern love circles in
space.
And our wings will grow stronger each and every
passing day.
Wings forever unclipped, knowing anytime we can
fly
to distant areas, alone, if need be,
but also, always knowing - we are able to return
and be together again as before,
playing for hours in ecstasy,
soaring above the turmoil and chaos of the world.
For we will create our own world,
free of wars and bickering,
free of destruction and unkindness.
For ours will be a world of peace, contentment
    -a world of love.

Heat of Love

And that cloudy night, you lit a candle.
The wick at first gave out a whisper as it touched the fire.
Then being devoured by the warmth
it poured forth a bright flame expelling the emptiness
as the flames tongue left its' fiery patterns on the walls
giving light to the darkened corners of my room
giving new meaning to the darkened comers of my soul.

And after time was spent
you bent over
and blowing out the flame
the wick again gave out a whisper

a whisper of fulfillment and peace

    a whisper of love.

And your love
poured
through my
prism
forming hundreds
of rainbows

The Handshake

We shook on it
We held hands.
We touched flesh and bone.
We touched wind, fire, rain
We touched trees, rivers, mountains.

We held all of life
in our palms
that day.

The sun rained fire that day.
The sky rained stars.
The clouds rained love.

I will not forget you
I know
- because I tried.

And the love flowed down like honey.

Time whispers of change for me;
of stability, security, commitment
of sailing on the moon
of flying on the sun
of singing on a star
of dancing on a cloud
of swimming on the fire
of running on the wind.

Time whispers - eternal love to me

(and you are the whisper I hear)

The Wall

And you don't even believe me!
You have no trust in me
no faith
I say, "I am in love with you."
But you ignore the screams of my heart.
You decide you can no longer be close.
You must not let yourself be hurt.
O please, don't be distant from me.
Please don't fly away!

I can sing you the songs of the rainbow.
I can fly you to the summit of the mountain.
I can show you clear, open air and sky,
I can take you to the land of peace
and flowing, sweet waters,

or
as you like –

I can build you a wall.
Yes, that is what you'd rather have.
A wall -
let's make it out of concrete, sturdy and secure.
A wall -
so you can protect your feelings.
Words and thoughts; no, don't let them out!
And don't let any outside force ever penetrate
your protective structure.

Yes, a wall - to shut the danger of pre-existing
pain,
        a wall - to shut out life.
a wall to shut out love.

Love Flower

O precious one,

Don't you know how special you are to me?
You are my flower in a sea of concrete.
You are my love in this world of hate.
And yes, I acknowledge my past
but I don't regret.
My past has led me to my present
and will lead me to my future -
a future I can see
-only with you.

The dawn sings of a new day.
My soul dreams
- on the road to my horizon.

The Circle

I awoke
and found myself lying on my back
gazing up at the sky, past pinon and cedar limbs.
A golden eagle soared overhead, close to the tree tops.
Small honey bees buzzed lazily in the warm sunshine.
My horse, tethered to a small cedar nearby,
swished his tail periodically at a pesky fly.
Minutes passed.
I just lay there and absorbed the sun,
the contentment and peace.
Then I felt you stir in my arms.
Your steady, regular breathing was interrupted
but was soon back to its' rhythmic pattern.
I felt your respirations on my chest,
your warm breath on my neck.
I gazed at your glowing hair, shining brightly in the sun.
The brightness, bringing forth dazzling highlights
of gold and amber.
I felt the touch of your hand, lying so lightly on my arm
the weight of your head on my neck and shoulder.
I once more gazed upward and spotted the eagle.
It now appeared as a lonely little dot high in the clouds,
circling as if endlessly in space endless
just as our love.

You are my shelter from the storm
my fire in the cold
my rain in the desert
my comfort in this world of pain.

I do not feel that anyone can tell the exact
moment when love is formed. As in filling a
vase, drop by drop, there is at last a drop
which makes it run over.

So in multitude of kindnesses, there is at last,
one which makes the heart run over.

We rode the ferris wheel of time
a time to laugh, a time to sing
a time to cry

a time to love.

You are my body's companion
but more importantly - my soul mate
my kindred spirit.

And yes,
this life can be as a fragrant, lush garden,
whose gate - is the human heart.

Dead End Street

You know your house of love
sits on a dead end street.
As I sullenly pull away from your curb
I think of all the sweetness
we have shared.
Yes, some bad times too
but the love always seemed to survive.

Yes, love lived on the dead-end street.

And as I drive away down the block
a stop sign comes into view.
I make my stop
lingering there at the comer.
thinking
where shall I turn?
where shall I now direct my course?

____

And is it not appropriate
to die on one's birthday?
It then becomes the birth of a new life.

Letting Go

The logger chops away at the towering pine.
With each swing the axe bites away
the core of the stately tree
until finally with the last blow of the sharp axe
tool - the pine lets go.

It drops to the earth
and strikes the ground.

This life is over but its' roots remain
and next year a new green sprout will emerge nearby.

The Camel Speaks

I have travelled the long journey
across the desert.
When I first began the trip
my hump was overflowing.
I had enough nourishment I thought
to last forever.
But the hot winds came.
The blazing sun withered all life
The ground grew parched
and all water disappeared.
When I finally arrived at my destination
my hump was also dry
I had no fuel to go on.

Days passed
and I grew very weak and tired,
until one night, by God's will
the sky broke open
and rain poured down.

I filled myself with life again
and on I walked

-to make another journey.

Consolidation

The wind calls your name to me.
At times I can feel your presence
I can touch your soul.
Your sweetness envelopes me,

And I ask:
as the mountain stream merges into the river
will the time ever be,
for your body and spirit to merge in my world?
and then unite yet another?

The Loom

You came into my life at a very necessary time -
you know,
My piece of tattered cloth was fast unraveling
The network of fibers once holding the pattern together
soon lie in a mound of disconnected, broken threads.
The brilliant colors of which had even rapidly faded.

Then you entered my world
and gently holding my structure
You stretched my injured soul on your loom
And from my tom discarded robe
you began to weave a splendid cloak of gold
a garment - very high in value
a garment of warmth, protection, friendship and
love.

And she came to me right at the peak of summer,
in the days of "the sun."
harvest time.
And from those sunny days she wove me a blanket
of golden warmth to protect me from the winter cold.
a blanket spun of Divine rays.
She nourished me as she does so many others
with her kindness and understanding.
But she treats me so very special.
I feel that I grow stronger every day.
My wings grow firm and well developed.
And what will I do when I can fly again?
Will I travel far?
This is my harvest time you know.
My life's harvest is beginning now.
And you helped make it so.
And so I wander - but alone I just travel
through empty space.
I still need your love to guide me.
    No, I will not fly away in solitary,
but meet you on the mountain top
to join you - in praise of the Sun.

A Token

It was like any evening - except one
as I drove down the rocky lane toward home.
The porch light was now visible
a sight always warming my heart
making me feel welcome and secure.
But then a dreaded thought flashed before me.
Will I truly be welcome this night?

After shutting my car door
I walked through the fresh snow toward the ole log house
I could now see tiny crystals of snow
falling lightly under the porch light.
The wetness touched my face as I opened the heavy door
and entered my home.
There in the fire light, I could see the silhouette
of a small figure, long hair flowing down her
shoulders and back. In her lap was a small dog,
a cat perched nearby, smoothing his fur.
She slowly bent forward and softly caressed the small
creature.
My love deepened as I observed her gentle movements.
Thoughts again flash:
Will others understand?
Will others open their minds and hearts
or will they be hurt in the process?

My trembling frame then made its way slowly to its
destination.
I approached the small figure.
Her face looked into mine.
Our eyes met, then twinkled with moisture
in the shadow of a subtle smile.
I reached toward her
I handed her - a token
I handed her
    my soul.

Eternal Flame

You are my eternal flame in this world of darkness
You are my rainbow in a blackened, cloudy sky
You are my sunshine in the deep of night
You are the refreshing rain in a parched and arid land.
I will never leave you - as the mountains never leave the sky
As the trees never leave the earth, I will root my soul to
yours.
Though separate entities we will be one with God
who has joined our sacred union.
Yes, even though your limbs may crack and your movement
be hindered in the wind, I will never leave your side,
for our spirits will move together.
What need is the physical then?
On Love, take us up where we belong
up where the eagles fly
up on mountains high where the clear winds blow.
Our love will soar then
as one with God and with each other.
And as I fly
I feel you and God
as the wind beneath my wings.

Spirit

O spirit of love, eternal flame
You who were once a tender herb on this earthly planet,
growing in the meadows of God's grace,
though your movement was often hindered in the wind
your form would bend into conformity with God's pleasure
your movement, your stillness were wholly directed by a hand
Divine.
And now the day has come. The great heavenly spirit has
reached
down and lifted you high, holding you in the palm of His hand
bearing you up to be in Paradise with Him.
And do not worry or fear
for your loved ones here remaining will never leave you.
As the mountains never leave the sky,
as the trees never leave the earth
we will root our souls to yours
and you will be for us as the wind is beneath the eagles wings
lifting us higher into the spiritual presence of the Divine.
Lifting us, encompassing us, as you have been encompassed
in God's tender warmth.
And now my love, now that the earth has claimed your limbs
now will you truly dance.
Now that the earth has claimed your voice
will you truly sing
And now without your earthly wings
will you truly fly.

Cross of Wood

Taken from an arid land
within a small grove of trees, they cut me.
I was shaped into two planks, 8 and 5 feet long
and let to dry in the sun on barren ground.
I weathered in this place for quite some time.
The grains of my wood often cracked under the stress of heat,
but I remained intact in this spot for several weeks.
Then one day I was lifted up.
My planks were bound together
I was carried and partly drug over a rough and rocky street.
The Man beneath my weight felt weak and shaky.
He fell with me three times that day.
Then I was thrown flat facing skyward and the Man who
carried me was thrown across my form.
Three nails were pounded into my wooden frame.
I felt something liquid run over and trickle down my
grains of wood where the nails pierced me.
I was brought up and pounded into the ground then,
into an upright position with the weight of the Man hanging
down
from me.
I felt this Man's body tremble. I heard His cries,
I felt His body jerk one final time.
His head fell to His chest before they lowered Him to the
ground.
They left me standing there for some time
intact, but stained in crimson red
with only a sign fastened to my wood.

Note of Sorrow

Oh world of pain,
World of greed and suffering
I long to tear the veils aside
Yes, do you hear His voice
as He cries through the heavens?
Do you see His tears?
Oh, when will He come again?
How long must we wait
for our Savior?

The Good Shepherd

Yes, a small black lamb caught in a brier bush
And I so desperately tried to get loose from the tangles
but the cockles kept sticking to my wool and holding me down.
I could not move,
And a feeling of hopelessness enveloped my soul.
Then I heard a faint sound in the distance, as of footsteps
drawing near.
I looked up to see two sandalled feet approaching me
then suddenly stop nearby.
I felt the briers then being tom away from my body,
being pulled away from my wool.
I felt two hands then hold me and pull me up,
two strong hands lifting me up toward the sky
there to gaze into the gentle, warm eyes
of my Savior.

The End
or - The Beginning

A New Day

And there will be a second creation's newest day
a world regenerated from decay
But in time, in God's own time,
we will once again be back in heaven's sunlight.
Life will again appear in new form.
New generations will again pass through life's many journeys.
And in the end again
all people and all things
will come home to their God.

Bom in St. Charles, Missouri in 1949, Sharon Ohlms spent
her childhood and young adult years in the surrounding
hills of this river town. After graduating in 1971 as a
physical therapist from the University of Missouri, she
moved to the countryside of Durango, Colorado to enjoy
the mountains and work in nearby hospitals. She lived
in a small log house and became interested in photography
at that time, and has since won recognition in several
professional contests in that area, with one entry
published in Photographer's Forum: The Best of Photo¬
graphy Annual 1981. As her writings and photography
reflect, Ms. Ohlms believes there is a harmony that flows
through all of life and through this harmony, one is able to
determine the reason of existence for all creation. There is a
spiritual factor in all of life and the beauty we see always
somehow returns to its one true Source. In 1991, Sharon
moved back to her home town of St. Charles to begin
another journey.

The previous pages portray glimpses of a life that you,
the readers, may identify with in some way as your own.